THIS BOOK
BELONGS TO:

_____

_____

DATE:

_____

GO GET 'EM, TIGER!

Words by Sabrina Moyle   Pictures by Eunice Moyle

ABRAMS APPLESEED | NEW YORK

Hey there, Tiger! You're

THE BEAST!

Now take a bite—the world's a feast!

Because you're

FIERCE.

A rising star!
You've earned your stripes.
You've come so far!

No matter who you choose
to be, you'll be

TERRR-IFIC.

Wait and see!

So view the world through

FIERY EYES.

Let it inspire, excite, surprise!

'Cause you've got

GRRR-IT

and smarts and heart.

You'll find your place.
You'll do your part.

You'll be humble—mind your claws.
When you tumble,
LAND ON YOUR PAWS!

You'll make mistakes. Things will go wrong.
And when they do, you'll carry on.

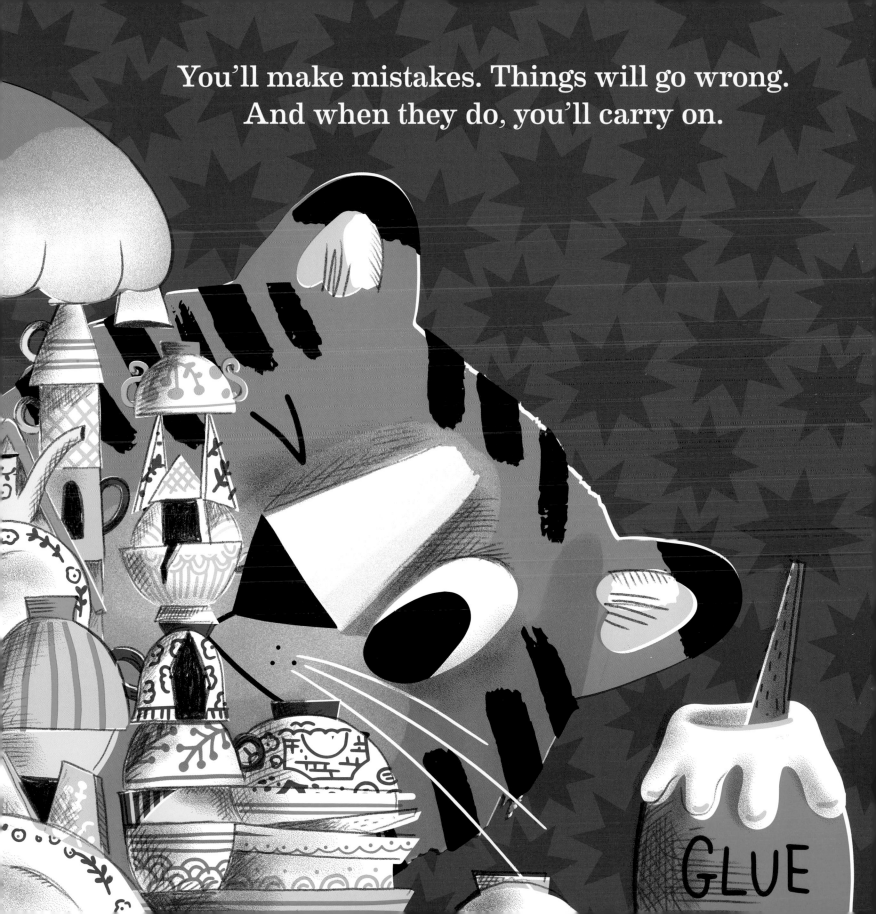

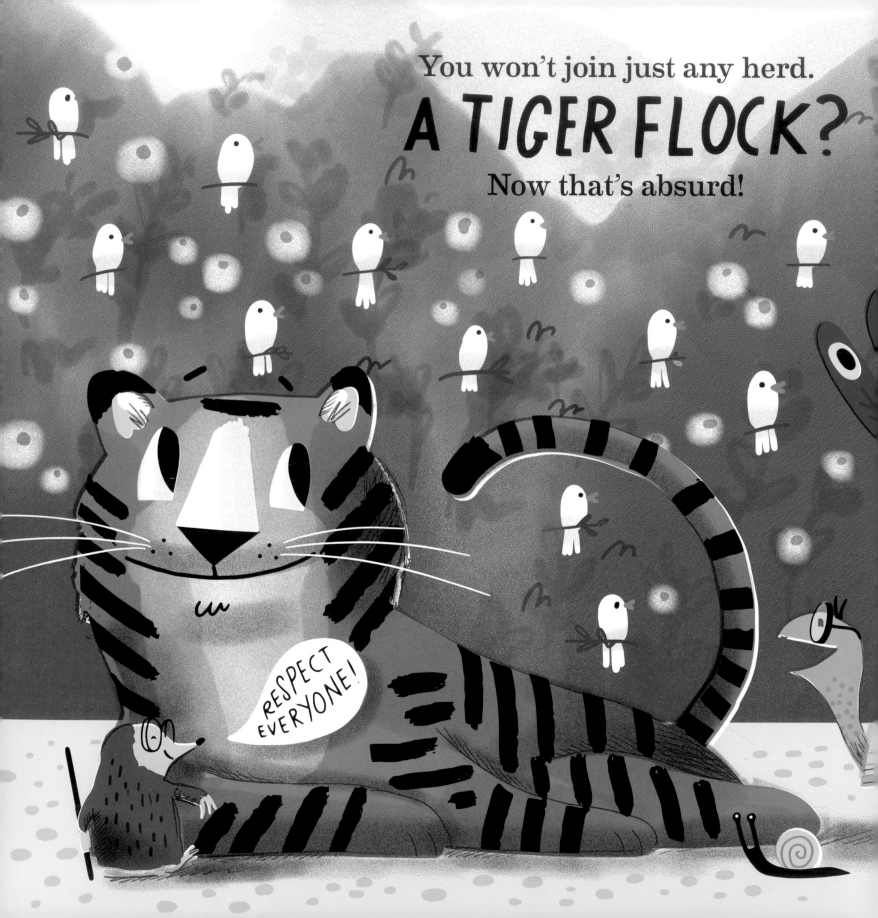

No, you'll make friends
with diffcrent beasts,
from the
STRONGEST
to the
LEAST.

You will see creatures who are stuck,
feeling lost, down on their luck.

To these new friends you'll lend a hand . . .

while keeping beat with

There will be days back in your den
when you won't know where to begin . . .

You'll take a break.
You'll take your time.
And soon you'll be
back in your prime!

You'll bring your calm
into the fray.
You will be bold—
you'll lead the way!

You'll use your strength to shine a light
on what is wrong and what is

RIGHT

To your spirit you'll stay true, never sorry to be you.
But **CHANGE YOUR STRIPES** if they don't suit you.
Dare to swap them—we'll salute you!

Go find some fun!

Go **POUNCE** and **PLAY!**

Hunt down delight in every day.

Make the most of every hour.
Unleash your

TIGER FLOWER
POWER!

Try to stop you? Don't you let 'em!

Your dreams are yours—

NOW GO AND GET 'EM!

To Alex, James, Julian, and William
—S.M.

To Daniel, Jude, and Imogen

—E.M.

The illustrations in this book were created digitally.

Library of Congress Control Number 2019944402
ISBN 978-1-4197-3964-4

Text and illustrations copyright © 2020 Hello!Lucky
Book design by Hana Anouk Nakamura

Printed and bound in U.S.A.
10 9 8 7 6 5 4 3 2

For bulk discount inquiries, contact specialsales@abramsbooks.com.

ABRAMS The Art of Books
195 Broadway, New York, NY 10007
abramsbooks.com